MOLLY PITCHER
THE WOMAN WHO FOUGHT THE WAR

Retold by
MARK CUNNINGHAM

Illustrated by
RICHARD MADISON

Cavendish
Square

New York

Mary Ludwig was born on a dairy farm in Trenton, New Jersey, in 1754. Her nickname as a child was Molly, and she became a household name as Molly Pitcher.

Molly was unlike most other girls her age at the time. Were she alive today, she would probably be called a tomboy.

Molly was a very energetic girl. She enjoyed working on the farm. She would dig the soil, sow the seeds, water the fields, harvest the grain, and even carry it to the granary. Some said she was strong enough to carry a three-bushel sack of grain on her back!

Molly knew that she could do a lot more with her life if she left her hometown and moved to a city. She was always on the lookout for an opportunity to move.

Her prayers were finally answered. When Molly was around thirteen years old, the wife of General Irvine visited Trenton.

Mrs. Irvine was to take a young girl home to Pennsylvania with her to help with the housework. When Molly heard this, she jumped at the chance. Molly went to meet Mrs. Irvine and begged her to take her along. Mrs. Irvine took an instant liking to the honest, outspoken girl.

Molly's parents did not want her to leave. They needed her help on the farm. But she did not want to spend the rest of her life on a farm. After many long arguments, she finally convinced her parents to let her go.

Molly went with Mrs. Irvine to her house. Molly worked very hard. She dusted, scrubbed, swept, and swabbed. She stitched and sewed too. She worked so hard that it was impossible to find someone who was better.

In a short time, Molly earned the respect of the Irvine family. She was treated not just as a valuable assistant but also as a member of the family.

What Molly liked best about living at the Irvines' were the war stories that the general would always tell.

Molly was very patriotic and loved her colony. "If girls could be soldiers, I would be one. I would go to war and shoot every one of the enemy," she once announced during dinner. Her eyes shone with determination.

General Irvine laughed. "You don't have to be a soldier to serve in a war," he said. "If you really want to help, you will get the chance someday."

He encouraged her, not wanting to shatter her dreams. In those days it was almost unheard of for a woman to fight.

But Molly held on to his words. She was convinced that she would get her chance one day. And when the moment arrived, she was determined not to disappoint her colony.

In the meantime, Molly had grown into a beautiful young woman. Many suitors pursued her, but she had already given her heart to William Hays, a handsome young barber in town. No one could resist her charm for very long, and William fell in love with her too. Soon, they got married in a small church.

Molly stopped working at the Irvines' and went to live with her husband. They bought a comfortable little house in the countryside. They lived there happily for a few years, until the American Revolution began. Every man was required to fight for the freedom of the country.

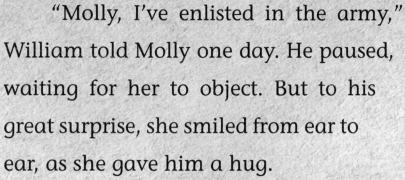

"Molly, I've enlisted in the army," William told Molly one day. He paused, waiting for her to object. But to his great surprise, she smiled from ear to ear, as she gave him a hug.

"Thank you so much!" she exclaimed. "Thank you William, for you have given me the great honor of being a soldier's wife," she said proudly.

Not once did Molly cry during the last few days that she had with William. In fact, when he was leaving, she cheerfully waved him goodbye.

Molly went to the Irvines' after William left. She worked there, sweeping, swabbing, and scrubbing.

One day, while hanging the washed clothes, she saw a horseman riding like lightning toward the house. "Perhaps he has some news of my William. It's been a very long time since he wrote to me," she thought.

She ran out eagerly to meet the horseman. She was correct. The horseman did indeed carry a letter from her husband.

My dear Molly,

Go with this man to your parents' farm. I have met them and they miss you. I am stationed close to your farm and would be able to visit with you if you were living there.

I miss you very much and would really like to see you.

Your loving husband,
William

Molly felt extremely happy when she read the letter. She missed her husband. She rushed in and asked Mrs. Irvine for permission to return to New Jersey.

"Of course you may!" exclaimed Mrs. Irvine, and helped Molly pack her clothes. In less than half an hour, Molly had tied up all her belongings into one small bundle and was on her way to her parents' farm with the messenger.

On reaching the farm, she was in for a surprise! Can you guess who was waiting for her there? William! She was overjoyed to see him safe and sound. After the initial surprise, they often met each other. Sometimes, he would come to the farm, and at other times, she would go to the camp.

When the soldiers went to fight, she would tend to the wounded. She would carry pitchers of water to the hurt or tired soldiers, which is how she got the name "Molly Pitcher."

One day, on reaching the campsite, she sensed that something was wrong. There was confusion at the camp. Everyone was riding out.

"What's going on?" she asked one of the soldiers.

"There's been a surprise attack at Morristown. We're all going there to fight. William's there too," he said.

"I'll join you!" said Molly, not wanting to miss out on the action.

The battlefield was a sad sight. Many of the soldiers had retreated. Others were lying on the ground, wounded. Molly tended to the wounded and gave water to as many soldiers as she could.

She saw a movement on the ground, the twitching hand of an injured man. It was Dylan, a friend of William's.

21

Dylan had fallen near his cannon. She saw a lit fuse a short distance from the loaded cannon. She had an idea. She took over his cannon, and fired the shot.

Unknown to her, Lord Cornwallis and the British were approaching. On hearing the cannon, they presumed that some men must still be manning the field. So they retreated.

Meanwhile, Molly carried Dylan back to her farm over her shoulder like she used to with the sacks of grain. She laid him on the bed and nursed him back to health. Once he was fit, he left and went back to fight.

Around this time, Molly gave birth to a beautiful baby boy. Many days and many nights passed without any news of William. Finally, she heard that he would be marching through New Jersey, toward New York. She was determined to take this chance to see her husband if she could.

So Molly went to the now-famous battle of Monmouth. The sight at the battlefield was a sad one. Many men were collapsing due to the heat. Even though she was going around, giving water to as many men as she could, it wasn't enough.

Suddenly, she heard a feeble whisper from behind her. "Molly." She turned around to find that her husband had collapsed from the heat.

"William!" Molly screamed, as she wiped his forehead with her handkerchief. She carried him to the shade under a tree. Just then, she heard the general give a command.

"Remove the cannon!" he said. "We have no one as brave as William to take his place!"

"No! Wait!" shouted Molly, running to the general's side. "Don't take the cannon away! I will work it."

For the next four hours she stood in the blistering heat, in her husband's place. She loaded and fired the cannon repeatedly. Finally, the battle ended. Only then did Molly leave her post and tend to William.

The general was very thankful to Molly. She was given the title of "Captain Molly," of which she was very proud.

Molly lived happily for the rest of her life, until she died at the age of seventy-three. She had fulfilled her dream. She finally got her chance to serve her country, and she served it bravely!

ABOUT MOLLY PITCHER

It is known that Molly Pitcher was an American soldier. But detailed, precise information about her got lost somewhere along the way.

The popular opinion among historians is that the stories of several young women who helped out during the American Revolution got merged and attributed to Mary Ludwig. All young women who carried water to the soldiers were called "Molly Pitcher." Besides, there are not many written accounts of her.

It is very difficult to say what is true or what is just a legend that has been added, as the story traveled down through the generations.

WORDS TO KNOW

Bushel: A bushel is a unit of measurement. It is equal to about eight gallons.

Cannon: A cannon was a huge gun used on battlefields.

Harvest: Once a crop had been grown, it had to be gathered and transported to the storehouse. This process of cutting and gathering the crop was known as harvesting.

Pitcher: A pitcher is a container that is used to carry water.

Troops: The army was divided into groups called troops.

TO FIND OUT MORE

BOOKS:

Burke, Rick. *Molly Pitcher (American Lives)*. Portsmouth: Heinemann (2003).

Rockwell, Anne. *They called her Molly Pitcher*. New York: Dragonfly Books (2006).

Stevenson, Augusta. *Molly Pitcher. Young Patriot*. New York: Aladdin (1986).

WEBSITES:

http://www.archives.gov/publications/prologue/1999/summer/pitcher.html

This is the link to an article that gives information about all the women who might have contributed to the legend of Molly Pitcher.

http://www.gardenofpraise.com/ibdmolly.htm

After reading about Molly Pitcher on this site, you can also solve fun crossword and word search puzzles.

http://www.readbookonline.net/readOnLine/48807/

This is a short story that you can read online. This story was written all the way back in 1917.

Published in 2014 by Cavendish Square Publishing, LLC
303 Park Avenue South, Suite 1247, New York, NY 10010
Copyright © 2014 by Cavendish Square Publishing, LLC
First Edition

Website: cavendishsq.com

This publication represents the opinions and views of the author based on his or her personal experience, knowledge, and research. The information in this book serves as a general guide only. The author and publisher have used their best efforts in preparing this book and disclaim liability rising directly or indirectly from the use and application of this book.

CPSIA Compliance Information: Batch #WW14CSQ

All websites were available and accurate when this book was sent to press.

LIBRARY OF CONGRESS CATALOGING-IN-PUBLICATION DATA

Cunningham, Mark, 1969-
Molly Pitcher/Mark Cunningham.
pages cm. — (American legends and folktales)
ISBN 978-1-62712-289-4 (hardcover) ISBN 978-1-62712-290-0 (paperback) ISBN 978-1-62712-291-7 (ebook)
1. Pitcher, Molly, 1754-1832—Juvenile literature. 2. Monmouth, Battle of, Freehold, N.J., 1778—Juvenile literature. 3. Women revolutionaries—United States—Biography—Juvenile literature. 4. Revolutionaries—United States—Biography—Juvenile literature. 5. United States—History—Revolution, 1775-1783—Biography—Juvenile literature.
I. Title.
E241.M7C87 2014
973.3092—dc23

Printed in the United States of America

Editorial Director: Dean Miller
Art Director: Jeffrey Talbot

Content and Design by quadrum
www.quadrumltd.com